The Everything Book

This book belongs to

_____

E
FLE

This book is for Indigo.

Henry Holt and Company, LLC
Publishers since 1866
115 West 18th Street
New York, New York 10011

Henry Holt is a registered trademark
of Henry Holt and Company, LLC

Published in Canada by Fitzhenry & Whiteside Ltd.,
195 Allstate Parkway, Markham, Ontario L3R 4T8.

Library of Congress Cataloging-in-Publication Data
Fleming, Denise.
The everything book / Denise Fleming.
Summary: A collection of simple works which introduce
colors, shapes, numbers, animals, food, and nursery rhymes.
1. Children's literature. [1. Literature—Collections.] I. Title
PZ5.F6 Ev 2000 [E] — dc21   99-53626

ISBN 0–8050–6292–0

First Edition—2000

Printed in the United States of America on acid–free paper. ∞

10   9   8   7   6   5   4   3   2   1

The illustrations were created by pouring colored cotton fiber through hand-cut stencils. Book design by Denise Fleming and David Powers

Learning

This is high, and this is Low,

Only see how much I know.

This is narrow, this is wide,

Something else I know besides.

Up is where the birds fly free,

Down is where my feet should be.

This is my *right* hand, as you see,

This is my left hand, all agree.

Overhead I raise them high,

Clap 1, 2, 3, and let them f l y.

—Anonymous

The Every

Henry Holt and Company • New York

thing Book

Book

Denise Fleming

Contents

Cock-a-doodle-do!
Hello! Good day!
Good
morning
to
you!

Five Little Chickens

Said the first little chicken
With a queer little squirm,
"Oh, I wish I could find
A fat little worm!"

Said the second little chicken
With an odd little shrug,
"Oh, I wish I could find
A fat little bug!"

Said the third little chicken
With a little sigh of grief,
"Oh, I wish I could find
A green little leaf!"

Said the fourth little chicken
With a sharp little squeal,
"Oh, I wish I could find
Some nice yellow meal!"

Said the fifth little chicken
With a faint little moan,
"Oh, I wish I could find
A wee gravel stone!"

"Now see here!" said their mother
From the green garden patch,
"If you want any breakfast,
you just come here and scratch!"
—*Anonymous*

13

Mealtime

spoon

toast

cereal

juice

carrots

banana

peas

egg

delicious!

yum!

milk

Fruit Colors

pink

red apple

orange orange

red strawberries

blue blueberries

watermelon

black
seed

yellow
pear

purple
grapes

green
grapes

purple
Plum

green
lime

17

Kitchen Toys

bag

cups

pan

cans

pot

spoon

19

Shapes

circle

triangles

rectangles

square

23

1 egg

2 eggs

3 eggs

4 eggs

5

crocodiles

Traffic Lights

"Stop," says the red light,
"Go," says the green,
"Wait," says the yellow light
Blinking in between.
That's what they say and
That's what they mean.
We all must obey them
Even the Queen.

—Anonymous

Choo-choo

This is a choo-choo train
Puffing down the track.
Now it's going forward,
Now it's going back.
Now the bell is ringing,
Now the whistle blows,
What a lot of noise it makes
Everywhere it goes.

—Anonymous

29

Two Little Blackbirds

Two little blackbirds
Sitting on a hill.
One was named Jack
And one was named Jill.

Fly away, Jack,
Fly away, Jill,

Come back, Jack,
Come back, Jill.

Two little blackbirds
Sitting on a hill.

—*Anonymous*

31

Spring

Summer

Fall

Winter

Robin's Nest

Here's a nest for Robin Redbreast.

Here's a hive for Busy Bee.

Here's a hole for Jack Rabbit—

and a house for me.

—*Anonymous*

37

Backyard

moth

fly

box turtle

toad

snail

butterfly

bee

dragonfly

caterpillar

ladybug

grasshopper

earthworm

ants

39

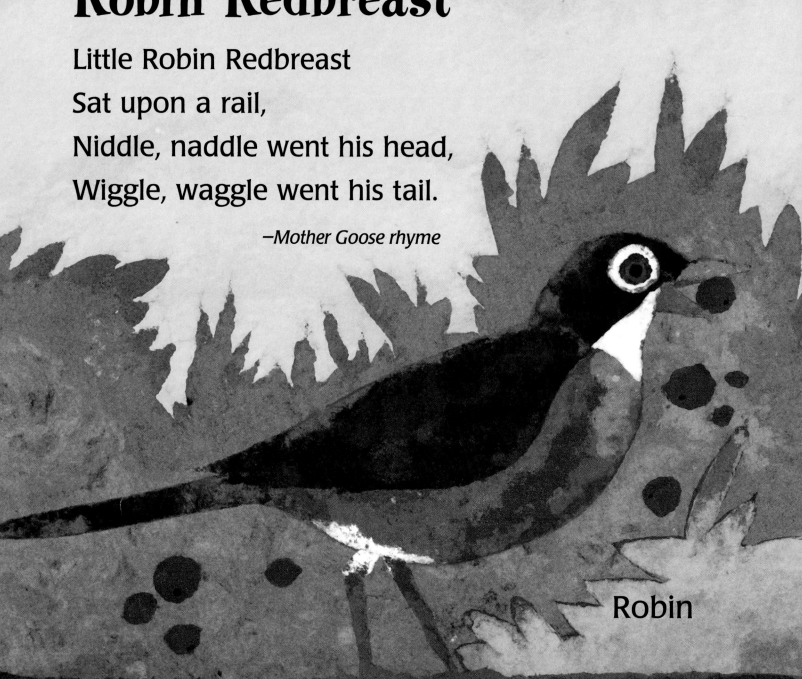

Robin Redbreast

Little Robin Redbreast
Sat upon a rail,
Niddle, naddle went his head,
Wiggle, waggle went his tail.

—Mother Goose rhyme

Robin

Pets

fish

kitty cat

guinea pig

bird

bunny rabbit

puppy dog

43

Head to Toe

head

hair

eyebrows

eyes

nose

ear

mouth

thumb

chin

fingers

fingers

shoulder

hand

chest

arm

wrist

elbow

toes

foot

foot

hair

head

eyebrows

eyes

nose

mouth   teeth

tongue   chin

ear

hand

fingers

hand

neck

arm

fingers

wrist

thumb

elbow

belly

leg

bottom

leg

foot

knee

ankle

foot

45

Peekaboo!

"Peekaboo,
I see you!"

"Now I do.
Now I don't.
Now I will.
Now I won't."

47

Tippy Toe

Tippy tippy tiptoe,
see how we go.

Tippy tippy tiptoe
to and fro.

Tippy tippy tiptoe
through the house.

Tippy tippy tiptoe
like a mouse.

—*Anonymous*

49

Faces

Waaaa!

Eew!

Humph!

Ha! Ha!

50

Favorite Places

under a table

behind
a chair

among
friends

on a lap

Mooly Cow

This mooly cow switched her tail all day,
And this mooly cow ate the sweet meadow hay,
And this mooly cow in the water did wade,
And this mooly cow chewed her cud in the shade,
And this mooly cow said, "Moo, the sun's gone down!
It's time to take the milk to town."

—*Anonymous*

56

57

Fireflies

Winking, blinking, winking, blinking,
See that little light.
Now it's here,
Now it's there,
Now it's out of sight.
Winking, blinking, winking, blinking,
Fireflies at night.

—Anonymous

Bunnies

"The bunnies now must go to bed,"
The furry mother bunny said.
"But I must count them first to see
If they have all come back to me.
One bunny, two bunnies, three bunnies dear,
Four bunnies, five bunnies; yes, they're all here.
They are the prettiest things alive,
My bunnies, one, two, three, four, five."

—Anonymous

Five little chicks
　　Without a peep
Close their eyes
　　And go to sleep.

Good night.

Count the Ladybugs

There are 119 ladybugs crawling or flying across the pages of *The Everything Book*.
Below is a list of pages on which ladybugs can be found and how many ladybugs are on each page.

Page 1 ——————————— 17 ladybugs
Page 2 ——————————— 17 ladybugs
Page 3 ——————————— 13 ladybugs
Page 5 ——————————— 1 ladybug
Page 7 ——————————— 1 ladybug
Page 8 ——————————— 1 ladybug
Page 11 ——————————— 1 ladybug
Page 13 ——————————— 1 ladybug
Page 15 ——————————— 1 ladybug
Page 16 ——————————— 1 ladybug
Page 18 ——————————— 1 ladybug
Page 20 ——————————— 1 ladybug
Page 23 ——————————— 1 ladybug
Page 24 ——————————— 5 ladybugs
Page 27 ——————————— 1 ladybug
Page 29 ——————————— 2 ladybugs
Page 30 ——————————— 2 ladybugs
Page 31 ——————————— 2 ladybugs
Page 32 ——————————— 1 ladybug
Page 33 ——————————— 1 ladybug
Page 34 ——————————— 1 ladybug
Page 36 ——————————— 1 ladybug
Page 39 ——————————— 1 ladybug
Page 41 ——————————— 1 ladybug
Page 43 ——————————— 1 ladybug
Page 44 ——————————— 1 ladybug
Page 46 ——————————— 1 ladybug
Page 47 ——————————— 1 ladybug
Page 49 ——————————— 1 ladybug
Page 51 ——————————— 1 ladybug
Page 52 ——————————— 1 ladybug
Page 53 ——————————— 1 ladybug
Page 54 ——————————— 1 ladybug
Page 55 ——————————— 1 ladybug
Page 57 ——————————— 1 ladybug
Page 59 ——————————— 1 ladybug
Page 61 ——————————— 1 ladybug
Page 62 ——————————— 17 ladybugs
Page 63 ——————————— 13 ladybugs
Page 64 ——————————— 1 ladybug

Bye-bye!